MW00890539

I know the Moon

Stephen Axel Anderson

illustrated by Greg Couch

Philomel Books

T he night creatures came to the mossy place in the deep wood, formed a silent circle, and saw the moon.

"I know the moon," said the fox.

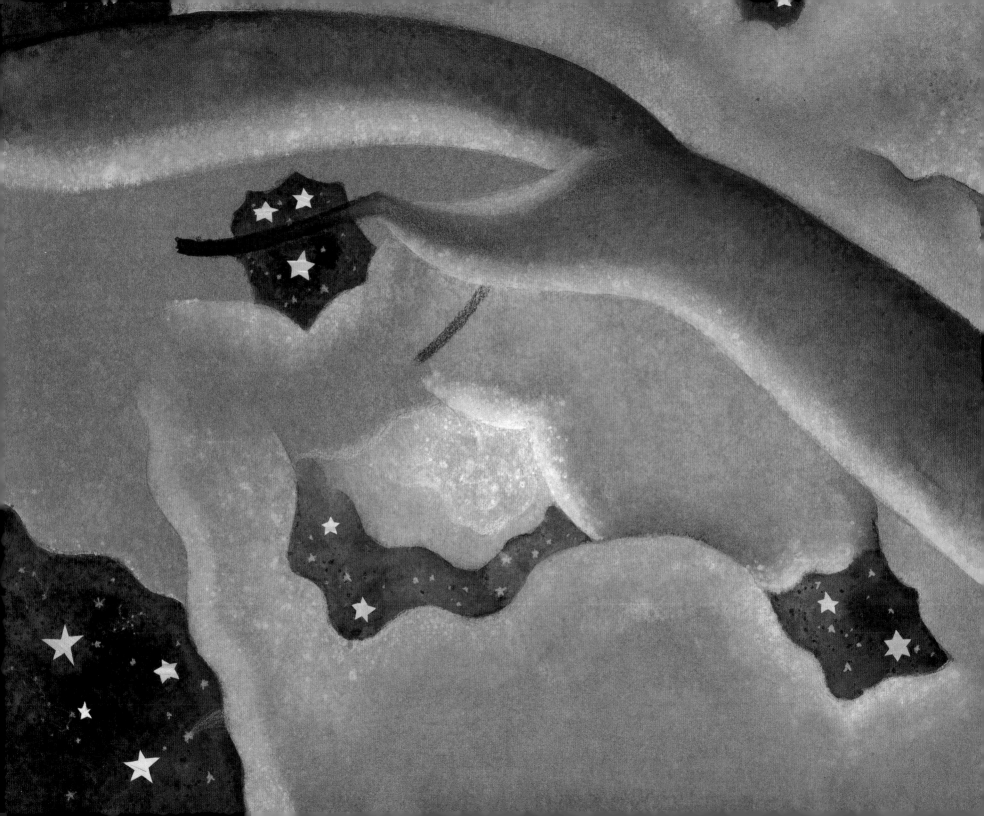

"I know the moon is a rabbit, swift and large and glowing. We play a merry game of chase, in and out of cloudy rabbit holes. No rabbit is her equal, and I'll not catch her soon.

"That is how I know the moon."

"The moon is not a rabbit,"
laughed the moth. "I know
the moon is a cocoon. A place
where moths of legend are
born and fly like stars to light
the sky." The great moth
moon-danced, light as air, and
bowed low on a golden leaf.

"Cocoon—that is how I
know the moon."

"No," said the owl, "it is not a cocoon. It is a window, cut through the night like the hollow of a tree. I see the light fly out and soar away and return to roost with the morning." The owl blinked slowly and stretched his wings.

"A window in a midnight room — that is how I know the moon."

"The moon is not a
window," said the mouse.
"It is a seed. Planted deep
in night soil, it blooms a sun-
flower by day and warms my
back, then slips to seed again
at dusk. It is a seed in endless
bloom.

"That is how I know the
moon."

"I know the moon is not
a seed," croaked the bullfrog.
"It is a lily pad. A golden lily
pad that glistens in every pond
and puddle. From there I can
admire my reflection and feed
on fireflies that wing about.

"A lily pad for froggy
croons — that is how I know
the moon."

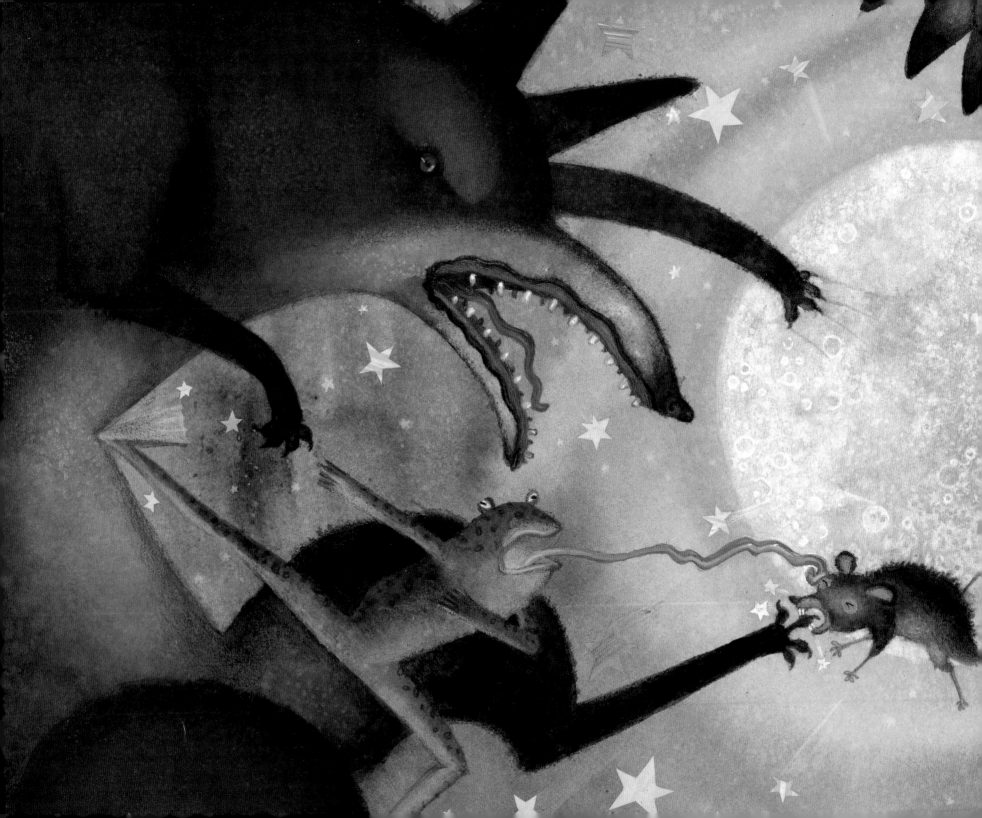

The animals, each convinced that he alone knew the moon, began to bicker. Soon their voices grew sharp and tangled, and glints of tooth and claw and angry eyes flashed in the night.

"Enough!" screeched the owl.

"There is but one moon, we shall have but one answer. The Man of Science! He reads the rings of trees, the stars at night, sunset colors, black on white. Surely he will know the moon."

So they trotted and fluttered and scampered and hopped and flapped their way to him.

The Man of Science lived alone with his thoughts in a tower high enough to almost touch the moon.

Almost.

He invited them in and seated them in a row according to width and breadth and height. In turn each animal told him of its moon, then pleaded, "Please tell me that *my* moon is right!"

The Man plucked a squarish book from his narrow shelf. "The moon, I understand, is a barren ball of sand. I know the width, I know the breadth, I know the height. It is dust, it is old, it is crust, it is cold. Facts and figures all in orbit! Read the moon! Then absorb it.

"To be sure, the moon is that and *nothing* more."

The night creatures crept cautiously to the book. They sniffed it, they squinted, they stared. The inky pages said not a word. Their moon simply was not there.

"You see," said the Man proudly, "it takes many words to know the moon." With that, he closed the book soundly. "I really thank you all for calling, but I really can't be dawdling, there's still so much to learn now— now good night."

The animals thanked him
politely and slipped sadly
into the darkness. The path
home was silent.

Far away now, the fox's voice swept away the cool night hush. "It takes more than words to know the moon, it must be chased and felt and seen. The Man says it's made of letters—I know it's more the spaces in between."

The other animals listened and understood.

"I know the moon is a cocoon," said the moth. "Not a ball of sand."

"A night window," said the owl. "Much more than dust."

"A seed in bloom," said the mouse. "Certainly more than crust."

"Not simply cold, but a lily pad," said the bullfrog.

The fox smiled. "A rabbit," he said, "but not a nothing."

"No," they said together. "Never a nothing."

The night creatures came
to the mossy place in the deep
wood, formed a silent circle,
and saw the moon.
Again.

For Paige, Brooke and Axel, moon-dreamers all.
And for Debbie, who watches over them. —S. A. A.

To my daughter, Emily, whose artwork continues to inspire me.
Thanks for all your help. —G. C.

Text copyright © 2001 by Stephen Axel Anderson.
Illustrations copyright © 2001 by Greg Couch.
All rights reserved. This book, or parts thereof, may not be reproduced in any
form without permission in writing from the publisher,
PHILOMEL BOOKS, a division of Penguin Putnam Books for Young Readers,
345 Hudson Street, New York, NY 10014.
Philomel Books, Reg. U.S. Pat. & Tm. Off. Published simultaneously in Canada.
Printed in Hong Kong by South China Printing Co. (1988) Ltd.
Book design by Semadar Megged. The text is set in Throhand Ink. The art for this book was
created with acrylic wash and colored pencil on two-ply museum board.
Library of Congress Cataloging-in-Publication Data
Anderson, Stephen Axel. I know the moon / Stephen Axel Anderson; illustrated by Greg Couch.
p. cm. Summary: When the animals cannot agree on just what the moon is, they turn to the
Man of Science to settle their dispute, but they are not satisfied with the answer he gives
them. [1. Moon—Fiction. 2. Animals—Fiction.] I. Couch, Greg, ill. II. Title.
PZ7.A55115 Iaak 2001 [E]—dc21 99-36027 CIP
ISBN 0-399-23425-X 10 9 8 7 6 5 4 3 2 1
First Impression